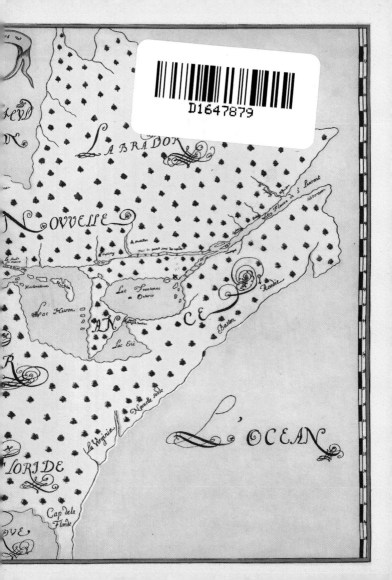

Bedtime Stories for the Edge of the World

ARP

Copyright ©2012 Shawna Dempsey and Lorri Millan
Arbeiter Ring Publishing
201E-121 Osborne Street
Winnipeg, Manitoba, Canada R3L 1Y4
www.arbeiterring.com

Printed in Canada by Friesens Corporation
Printed on paper with 10% PCW

Design by Lisa Friesen, WAG
Calligraphy by Nicole Coulson
Proofreading by Heidi Harms and Finn McMahon

Manuscript created with support to the artists by the City of Winnipeg
through the Winnipeg Arts Council, and the Winnipeg Art Gallery.

ARP acknowledges the financial support of our publishing activities by
Manitoba Culture, Heritage, and Tourism, and the Government of Canada
through the Canada Book Fund. ARP acknowledges the support of the
Province of Manitoba through the Book Publishing Tax Credit and the Book
Publisher Marketing Assistance Program. We acknowledge the support of
the Canada Council for our publishing program. With the generous support
of the Manitoba Arts Council.

LIBRARY AND ARCHIVES CANADA CATALOGUING IN PUBLICATION

Dempsey, Shawna
      Bedtime stories for the edge of the world / Shawna Dempsey, Lorri Millan.

ISBN 978-1-894037-82-2

      I. Millan, Lorri II. Title.

PS8607.E573B43 2012   C813'.6   C2012-905489-5

CONTENTS

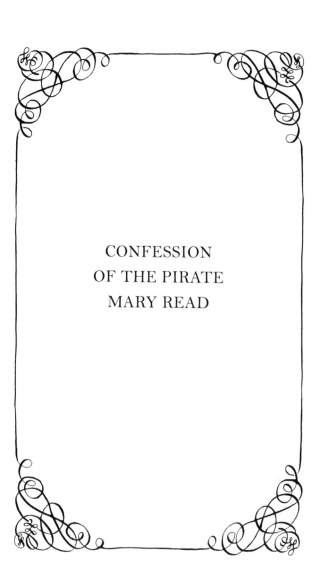

CONFESSION
OF THE PIRATE
MARY READ

HERE are always Moments in Battle when the Smoke, Gore, and Din give way to Order and a Path opens, a Plan reveals itself, and the mathematical Perfection of Life and Death and Booty is lit from within, proclaiming Action as the Only Course, the Only Way to live or die, the Only Thing that makes us worthy of being called by our Names. That perfect Moment of Vengeance, Mercy, or Pillage. That Maiming Jab or Fatal Thrust, that Grab-and-Run, Fire-The-Cannon, Starboard-Ho. It is Beauty and Purpose, at those times, to be a Pirate. The Sound of my Fist striking Skull, the Smell of Sweat licking Skin, the Fires of Hell at my Musket's command.

Jewels and Silks are lovely, later, to buy a Good Meal and Rumbullion. Even to wear—to out-finery each other—such a Crew of Molly Men and Tribades are we! But for each of us it is the Movement of our Limbs, the Doing of Something, the Forcing of our Will upon a World that gave us up as Useless before we were born: that, that is the Love of Being; that is the Love of being a Pirate.

Amidst the Roar of Gunpowder I saw her and she was like that, I swear, all Calm, all Action, all Certain. As big as two Men and stripped to the Waist, red Hair streaming down Back and Chin and, I would find later, down Cunny. I jumped from the Deck of King George's Ship and hollered, "I'm with you, Anne Bonny, don't kill me." Laughing as I leapt. Knowing what was behind me (the Life of a Navy Seaman, the Hiding of my She-Sex, and before that Hunger) would be banished by our Banshee Call and what I was leaping toward was her Arms, her Bed, the Force of my own Body.

She caught me to her Chest, and prodded a Dagger to my Gullet. Above the Thunder she shouted, "I'll slit your Throat dare you cross me!" I realized then that I had been white-livered all my Life and I kissed her, tempting Knife Point and not caring, for I felt free and knew, come what may, it was of My Own Making.

Anne Bonny spit my Tongue from her Mouth, sliced a Button from my Coat, and carried on with the Mayhem. I realized I had been spared her Blade, and hoped this showed some Affection. Why she took my Button I did not know, but a British Jacket did me no advantage as a Pirate. Surely I would have been run through with a Bandit's Sabre had I not stripped bare to my Titties and, thus Unfettered, I began to fight against those with whom I had once served, arousing Surprise with my Womanliness. Even Anne's attention was caught, and she near lost her Life with Distraction.

Soon the Villains swarmed the Deck led by the Navy Captain himself. He would have struck Anne from behind, had I not the Fury to throw Musket Balls beneath his Boots, upending the Prig to the Planks. I flew at him then and gutted the Gentleman, paying thanks to all the Men who had owned me. Anne and I often laughed about that Moment, the Brit's Eyes on my Flopping Woman Parts as I struck and gored him. Whether Terror or Pleasure filled his Last Breath we could not say but, either way, it was not the Heroic Ending he had imagined.

Anne Bonny has kept my Button in her Pocket these Three Years since, rubbing it bright between her Fingers. When we quarrelled, the Brass Token was tossed on Deck and even Overboard twice, but we always found it again through Luck and Stubbornness, and were able to carry on to Greater Adventure. We both knew our Lives and Happiness could be Lost as easily as that Button, and that to be a Pirate was to Steal all that could be carried and all that cannot. Time is taken from us if we do not take it for ourselves—it is so very Sweet and Fleeting.

Jailors and Judges have spun many Tales about the Night we were Caught, and ought to have their Tongues cut off for their Jabber. His Majesty's Men were neither Cunning nor Brave. Our Men were simply sodden.

It is heavy Work, the Thieving and Running, and the Salt Air makes a Body thirsty. We filled many Nights with our Merry Making Fun, and that last one won't soon be forgotten. The boys preened in Calico, threw Knives and Dice, and danced until they were hobbled. Songs were sung and Kegs were smashed, and All were Handsome and Jolly. The Ship, Sea, and Stars never looked so Bright, nor did my own Anne Bonny. She and I were Well-Sated with Drink and slept fast 'til we heard the Cannon's Thunder.

Oh, the Miserable Sight that awaited us in the pink Dawn's Mist. One of the King's Galleons lurked a Stone's throw aft, and our Fine Crew was a Wreckage of Vomit and Snoring. We tried to wake them then with Curses and Kicks, but they were good for nothing but Groaning. We gathered their Pistols and rushed to the Falconets, but before we could load the Cannons, the Devils calmly extended a Plank and crossed to where we were standing.

Two women against the British Navy is hardly a fair Fight, and we trounced them thoroughly! Dozens of Tricorned Lads were left Bloodied and Broken and mewling like Kittens. So it is no surprise that Anne escaped, and it was only by Deviousness that I was Captured.

My Captain threw herself into the Sea, a Breathing Tube hidden 'round her Waist, and I would have joined her there to swim to our Hidden Ship had they not held me fast to rape my Person.

I bear my Mates no Malice for this, nor none to Anne, neither. In Choosing to be Pirates we must Save Ourselves, too, whenever we are able. We have our Ways 'neath the Jolly Roger, a Flag more fair than their Standard.

The Cross of St. George runs bloody and brutal, leaving those without Coin to Perish. Like the poor Fellows on a Slaving Ship, its Subjects are thrown from Slop Pail to Trough, chewed up and shat out, Breakfast for a few fat Piggies. That is the way of Society; that is the way of Mother England.

And they wonder why we risk the Noose! That Necklace is my Fair Due, and prettier still than the Hands of Father, Master, Husband, and all of them that would have choked the Life out of me far sooner than this. They say that I will be hung like a Dog, but nay, I will take Hanging like a Woman who is herself a Master, and wish it to be a Spectacle, with Treats for Children and Small Beer for Ladies. Let them all see what I have done and before the Hood is put on my Head I will say out loud, "It was worth it."

No, a brave and bonny Band we were, and no finer Friends a Person can have than those who will cut a Throat or hold your Swag while you burn and plunder. I hope to God I meet my Mates in Hell, for I do miss our Merriment. Perhaps I will get the Brimstone roaring, to make it warm and welcome.

The only one I do not wish to see there is Anne Bonny. I pray she keeps sailing as long as she is able; I pray she can sail on forever. It would be a great Comfort to know that Someone, one of us, could evade their Bonds; that she might remain Free, catching the Others who dare to leap; that there is one safe Place (the Sea!), one Person who does not submit, who lives our Lives as they should be. It would help me in this Passing, this Dying, to know our Good Works will continue.

Ha! The Liberation of Goods from Sailing Ships!

I love you, Anne Bonny, all the more knowing you won't come back for me. I have wanted you as sure as I have breathed. And wanted this Life that we made. It has birthed me, Mary Read; Anne has birthed me; and I have birthed myself, with my every Word and Deed and Murder. Now I await my Fate without Fear, Breasts bared like a Woman and Teeth bared like a Man, asking no Forgiveness.

That is my Shriving. Leave me be.

Anne Bonny and Mary Read pirated the Bahamas together for three years in the early 1700s. At a time when the wearing of men's clothing was punishable by death and all women were owned (by father, brother, husband, master, or state) and could be sold at auction, Anne Bonny rose to the rank of Captain of her own pirate ship. She succeeded by being more intelligent and more brutal than her male counterparts. The fact that she was able to command respect from her crew is

perhaps explained by a pirate culture that allowed wayward and deviant behaviour. For example, Pierre Vane was a known homosexual and professional hairdresser, drawn to piracy by his love for opulent booty, especially fine fabrics. Likewise, Calico Jack (originator of the skull-and-crossbones flag) was infamous not only for his brightly coloured trousers, but also a taste for men. Both captained their own ships.

Rogue vessels and ports were known refuges for murderers, thieves, deserters, and anyone else who managed to survive and escape the strict social, racial, religious, and class codes of the time. This included women fleeing ownership, which they did in numbers greater than we can imagine. Hundreds of navy sailors were "unmasked" as cross-dressing women and no doubt more went undetected. Some, like Mary Read and Anne Bonny, preferred to risk adventure while maintaining their female identities, and embraced a life of piracy and liberty on the high seas.

Mary Read avoided the noose because of pregnancy and is believed to have died in prison in Jamaica. Anne Bonny escaped and, despite a high price on her head for arson, murder, conspiracy, and the freeing of slaves from ships, was never re-apprehended.

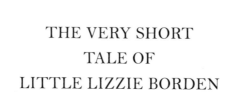

THE VERY SHORT
TALE OF
LITTLE LIZZIE BORDEN

HO is to say she did it? It is so unnatural, a child taking the lives of her parents. They say she loved her Pap, loved him dearly, and that he loved her dearly, too. It's unfathomable why she would, of all things, chop him up. Not to mention unladylike, and Little Lizzie, despite her temper and strange moods, had grown into what she was raised to be: a lady, or as much a lady as her Pap's tight purse strings would allow. She did good works, went to church, and was always beautifully turned out. Murder is almost too much to consider....

And yet we more than consider, we know. Despite the plea, despite the verdict, despite the fact she got off scot-free, we know in the lowest pit of our guts she did it, all right, she did. She lifted that hatchet (for an axe it was not), and handily murdered her stepmother and belov'd Pap. We know she did it as surely as if we had done it ourselves. All of us could have, wanted to, too: shatter, chop, hack. And ladylike, we wouldn't sweat. Not a hair would be out of place. Our buttons wouldn't even pop until later, in our haste to remove the bloody dress and undergarments so as to be presentable for all who came to gawk.

We know what it's like to have anger crackle from neatly ragged curls. We know the burn of madness bore of wool stockings on a summer day, flatly placed-down table settings, and love and obedience owed to our Fathers and Missuses and Paps.

There is no doubt as to the murderer. And though we make a show of asking, "Why, why?" there is no doubt as to the reason, either.

SHE was not the first born so shouldn't have been so difficult, but she came out feet first, screaming, and looking for all the world like the devil himself. Or so said the Irish washerwoman who attended Little Lizzie's mother. Little Lizzie's mother herself was too busy vomiting to notice. The pain had been too much, and the washerwoman, though kind, was as helpful and skilled as befit her fee, 15¢ an armful for laundry, and pitiful more for catching the babe.

Little Lizzie's mother had cried as she laboured, "I hate him, I hate him, I wish him dead." But it was just the pain talking, the washerwoman knew. What mother doesn't hate her man as she pushes and pushes for hours, and for what? The little red, wrinkled things that come out of us then break our hearts. The washerwoman had birthed fourteen of her own, three dead right off the hop, four that were taken by fever, two in mill accidents so bad there wasn't much left to collect, and one that was trampled by a horse. That left four, and the only one she could rightly keep track of was the youngest, in gaol up in Salem.

Young Mrs. Borden had a lot to look forward to, she did. But she wasn't as tough as the Irish washerwoman. Mrs. Borden's heart couldn't take even the everyday breaking.

Mrs. Borden died when Little Lizzie was but three years old.

The Very Short Tale of Little Lizzie Borden

LITTLE Lizzie Borden was a small child with a stump nose and two rows of sharp, white teeth. She lived with her progenitor, a Mr. Borden, his wife, and her older sister, the love of her life, Emma, quiet and pretty and smart. She had other loves, too: the servant girl Maggie, the dog Snowball, and the old woman who came once a week and took laundry. Even though Little Lizzie Borden was only five, she called this assortment of female friends, family, and animals her lovers, for she loved them, and knew what that meant. She would hear of no ill spoken against them. She would make mud dolls in their likenesses and eat them right up. And she would, when she could, bite their very selves with her sharp, white teeth. Just because it felt so good. That Little Lizzie was a peculiar child.

ADULTS got in Lizzie Borden's way. They stopped her from putting things in her mouth: her fingers, bug parts, mud. They didn't answer her questions, or, worse yet, answered them unsatisfactorily. Adults brushed Lizzie's hair, made her go to bed when there was still light in the sky, and punished anyone—especially Lizzie—who was really going to have some fun. What was fun to adults was incomprehensible to Lizzie: reading and sewing by the light of the lamp. "Stop that," she would yell, and kick her small heels, too. Lizzie was a bad girl.

Her bedroom adjoined that of her parents by a door. Through that door Lizzie could enter the world of Mr. and Mrs. Borden, and see them go about their adult ways. She would slip inside in the morning to watch her father flip and flail his tie to a knot. She would examine her stepmother's undergarments that stood by themselves and had more personality unoccupied than with Mrs. Borden within. Sometimes she would spy on Mr. Borden in his undertaker's suit, on top of his wife rocking up-down.

Invariably, Little Lizzie's presence startled her parents, but their chiding and spanks did not keep her away. She was bored by the senior Bordens, but there was not much else to look at. Little Lizzie liked to watch. She paid attention and learned, by example, how to tie a necktie.

In desperation, the parents of Little Lizzie Borden installed a stout lock between the rooms. It was the heaviest quality money could buy, and although old Borden didn't like to part with his cash, no amount was too great to keep out Lizzie's eyes.

This lock was the first, but there would be many to follow on all of the rooms, each one newer and stronger and more impenetrable than the last. As many as three laced each door to its jamb. They were not intended to keep safe the fortune of Borden the undertaker, as papers would report, but to keep in her place his Lizzie.

LITTLE Lizzie Borden tried to alter the course of history, to avoid picking up that hatchet and breaking not one commandment but two.

The first sixteen years of her life were devoted to learning about places as far from Fall River as you could get, making her limbs strong enough that she could someday run away, and generally being disagreeable.

If you gave her a ball she'd let you know in plain language it was a bat that she wanted. If you complimented her long, red hair she'd be apt to go to the barn and hack it off. She demanded mutton for breakfast and porridge for supper, jam with her meat and gravy with her bread. She had at least one immovable opinion about everything in her world, and many other things besides.

Little Lizzie practised witchcraft. Oh, that's not what she called it. She looked at coincidence and happenstance and tried to repeat the variables to achieve the same effect. If the cock crowed when the smell of ammonia was in the air, just as Lizzie's stepmother took a tumble down the stairs, well … Lizzie would scrub the landing every morning for a week and then pull the tailfeathers from the rooster: in an effort to get a sound from him, in an effort to repeat the fall, in an effort to make her will felt, to make something happen where not much happened at all.

These experiments were conducted with a guilty conscience. Little Lizzie knew that hexes and hopes were at odds with God. God frowned on hope, and rewarded hard work and blind faith. So she was not surprised on New Year's Day, 1876, when she was sixteen and much too old to believe in hocus pocus, much too old to be so disagreeable, that she glanced at her drawers and saw blood. No one had told her to expect this visitor. A woman in 1876 was more apt to claim to have malaria than admit to, to speak about, the curse. No one warned Lizzie. There was nothing in good taste anyone could say.

And really it didn't matter. In the pit of her newly aching womb Lizzie knew. It *was* the curse, her curse. She was a woman now and there would be no more trying to alter fate. Skipping backwards wouldn't work, faraway places didn't want her, there was no longer any point in arguing about bats and balls, when to eat gravy or jam. There was nothing to be done but sit, do fancy work by the light of the lamp, and wait.

The sight of blood pushed Lizzie Borden to the ground, made her eyes roll back, made her tongue roll back, made her speak in tongues. Dr. Bowen called it a fit, and it would be the first of many. Mrs. Borden, Emma, and the woman who took laundry guessed that Lizzie was merely unwell, in the womanly way.

HERE ends the beginning of the story of Little Lizzie Borden. There is really not much middle, besides the waiting, and we all know the ending. The beginning is really the best part of the tale. It is when anything can still happen; when we can believe Lizzie will have adventures, save herself and the day; when we can hope that everything will turn out, after a few twists and turns, just fine.

Instead Lizzie and Emma finished school, went to church, collected stamps, and counted stitches. They continued to sleep in the same room they had shared since Lizzie's birth, decades ago now. Holding hands in bed at night, they would talk of Boston, San Francisco, Red Indians, and Arabs. "I'd sell myself tomorrow, if I weren't too old for harlotry," Lizzie would snort. At the age of thirty-eight, her hair still escaped its bounds, her tears still sprang unbidden, and improprieties still spilled from her lips.

"Hush," Emma would caution. "Someone might hear you." But no one did.

Throughout her life, Lizzie Borden (1860–1927) maintained that she did not murder her parents on August 4, 1892. Despite being acquitted of the crime, speculation continues to the present day. One theory

holds that Lizzie was guilty as charged, and that she performed the parricide while in a fugue state—of which she had no memory—provoked by temporal lobe seizures associated with menstruation. Alternate suspects in the crime have been posited, including Bridget Sullivan, the family's maid, and William Borden, Robert Borden's illegitimate son.

With their inheritance, Lizzie and her sister Emma purchased a fashionable new home where Lizzie became infamous for hosting raucous, all-woman parties. Eventually, this caused the siblings to quarrel and Emma left to live with her close friend, nurse Alice Buck.

Lizzie lived out her years as a spinster and, upon her death, she willed the bulk of her sizable fortune to the Fall River Animal Rescue League. Emma died nine days later.

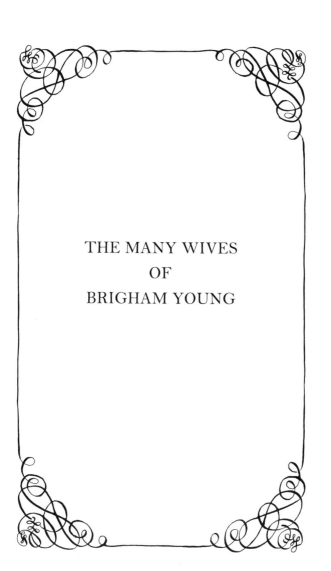

THE MANY WIVES
OF
BRIGHAM YOUNG

O hear people on the outside talk, it was as if all the womenfolk in Salt Lake were attendant on his poor, wee cock. And of course Brigham's version wasn't much better. He was saving us from the horrors of the charnel house or, worse yet, spinsterdom. But that wasn't it either. It wasn't slavery or salvation. It was both.

To live as one among many—one wife amidst more than fifty others—is not to be married to a man. Oh, there was the inconvenience of the man. But the chalk marks he made on my door and the grunting that followed were easier to bear than all that praying, and at least brought the blessing of children. I can't rightly complain of the housework either. Extra hands make light work, and between us wives and the young we begot, we had hundreds of them. Hands, that is. Hardworking ones.

It was certainly no Sultan's court. To those ladies with their pantaloons of real silk and fruits that spilt juice, our lives would have seemed mean indeed. The desert got into our ears and eyes, our stockings, our food, even salted our dreams. It almost killed us to get there, and what's worse, that is where we stayed. But the women's quarters… We didn't have pretty things, but it was an oasis.

After my wedding, Brigham spent a fortnight in my room. But once he had taken his fill and his leave the other wives came to me, and I was readied as if for marriage. They prepared me as it is described in the Bible, feeding me, plaiting my hair, washing my body and rubbing it with oil, washing my woman-parts, too. Then each one told me why I was loved by her, each one kissed my mouth, and each one touched a bit of me. Some stroked my head, some licked my toes, some suckled my breasts, and to be suckled by a woman makes you think of your child and your mother— more!—and there is surely nothing sweeter. For hours I was caressed by seventeen mouths. My bladder let go and they caught my water in their seventeen mouths. Those seventeen mouths made something happen that I didn't understand, but have never stopped wanting. And then they each slapped me, and kissed me, and the sucking began again, oh.

Their tongues and fingers found their ways to so many places. Everywhere that was forbidden. But by the sting of their switches and the slap of their palms on my bare bottom and thighs, my cheeks and breasts, I knew I was forgiven.

Many times I was cared for in this way, and many more I cared for others.

I've heard it said that Emmeline Free was Brigham's favourite, but that's a lie, too. She was our favourite. Number twenty-one, three after me. So beautiful, so tiny, so fair and perfect. Freckles. She could say a few words and make us all laugh like firecrackers, or say a few words and make us all cry. We all loved her and you would, too. She was born to be loved.

None of us would drink milk for a week. We would collect it up in a can in the cellar and when we had enough we would warm it, fill the steel tub, and bathe Emmeline like royalty. Her white limbs in that white, warm soup, and all our fingers swimming towards her like fishes! With our mouths we'd lick her dry. Nothing tasted more like heaven. It was a blessing that Emmeline fell into disuse by Brigham. Then Emmeline had more time to be loved.

Like most marriages, ours was not without argument. There were times when Emmeline wanted to be left alone, and that hurt the twenty-five, thirty-five, forty of us terribly. (The numbers kept changing, I often lost track.) And she could be angry and jealous, too, accusing us of looking at another, when really we had eyes only for her. We could fight about little things, where to plant the squash, how to dress a table. Sometimes it felt that our love was too big, and it snuck out in mean words. But usually it didn't take too long to make it right again.

That is, until Ann Eliza arrived. Ann Eliza was a black-haired, black-hearted trouble-maker. For reasons none of us knew, she didn't like Emmeline one bit. She put lizards in her bed, hid sharp pins in her needlework. She was all hatred and bile, and just that one drop of vinegar, one wife among fifty, turned our great love sour. We were no longer one body loving Emmeline. A disease had set in. The fingers and lips we had loved with ached like they'd fall off. Our hearts broke and we were unkind. Woman to woman we were hurtful and cruel, to none more than beloved Emmeline.

Ann Eliza asked the Justice for a divorce as much as or more from the rest of us as from Brigham. We could barely imagine it and, of course, Brigham couldn't allow it. He fought it on the grounds that someone can't legally be married to more than one person. Ann Eliza couldn't divorce him, he argued, because they'd never been legally wed. And where did that leave the rest of us fifty-one? Living sinfully. Brigham won, making us whorish and dirty in the process.

He died soon after, less than a day before the passing of our true love Emmeline. Brigham was ancient, but typhoid took Emmeline, along with six of our children that season. It was a funny thing, them both laid out in the parlour, man and wife. We grieved plenty, but weren't even sure what we were grieving for.

Brigham left everything—our home, the food in our pantry, and the clothes from our backs, if he could have arranged it—to his almighty church. Our own selves were even willed away, each wife beside the name of a man to whom we would be sealed, lest any of us escape heaven. But worst of all, he said we would all be split apart, the whole community, to begin again in new, more godforsaken places.

Almost as an afterthought, Emmeline's will was read. As was custom, she should have left all that she owned—pitiful, really—to her husband. And she did. "I hereby bequeath all that I own to my husband, Ann Eliza."

The lawyer looked confused. We all looked confused. Ann Eliza looked as sour and hard as ever, but you could tell even she was surprised. Ann Eliza had never shown an ounce of kindness to Emmeline, and yet Ann Eliza was the one to whom Emmeline left her dresses and ribbons and sewing box.

"That's not right," someone said. Maybe we all said it. There was murmuring all around. But in the eyes of the law we all knew that none of us had a husband and besides, the lawyer said, she could leave her things to whomever she named.

That night Ann Eliza collected up Emmeline's things. A fortnight later she was gone. She'd hired four of the young men who hang about, too weak to marry, too old for school. She bought horses and conveyance and supplies for travelling. The day she left she sat up proud on the wagon. No one came out to see her off. We all watched from inside, our palms pressed to the glass, each asking, "Why wasn't I the one chosen?"

Our faith tells us that the Prophet received the word of God on golden plates, which he translated and then returned to the angel. But I know now the angel never got them back. Who wouldn't keep gold close? Unbeknownst to us, despite the hunger and the hardship, Brigham had held those plates safe, hidden in Emmeline's sewing box.

Dear Emmeline. She must have known, about the gold and more. She must have known that Ann Eliza was the only one with the courage to leave. Or call it spite. Certainly Ann Eliza was the only one who could melt down the word of God for her own purposes. I imagine her sometimes in a Sultan's palace of her own, eating sweets and listening to music. I imagine Emmeline is with her, reclined on a velvet bench. But of course that's crazy.

I think about it as I walk. I'm hitched to the wagon again. It's too much work to keep my head up. I face my feet, and that way I feel I'm moving forward, though I know part of every sandy step is a slide back. Some of us are moving to the new country of Canada. We carry the Book of Mormon, some tools, and household things. Not much else. At fifty-six, I'm an old woman. Called to do missionary work. I don't mind. I've heard the land to the north is ruled by a queen, Victoria. I wonder if

she keeps a harem, or takes baths in thick cream?
If I could touch her someday, I'd know by the feel
of her skin.

*When colonists came to North America, they were
struck by the Edenic quality of the landscape. This pri-
mal awe, combined with separation from traditional
Christian churches in Europe, led to distinctly North
American expressions of faith (personally interpreted
Bible-based theology) and the formation of entirely
new denominations. These include the Church of Jesus
Christ of Latter-day Saints, whose adherents, known
as Mormons, have faced mistrust, discrimination, and
oppression since the church's inception in 1829.*

*Brigham Young (1801–1877) was the second
leader of the Church of Jesus Christ of Latter-
day Saints. Although the faith's founder, Joseph
Smith, ordained the practice of polygamy, it reached its
zenith under Young's leadership. Over his lifetime,
Young had a total of fifty-five wives. These included*

Emmeline Free, who bore him ten children, and Ann Eliza, who famously sued for divorce and became an anti-polygamy activist. Polygamy was abolished by the Church in 1890 to conform to American law.

All world religions, including the New World faiths, contain elements that, to the nonbeliever, read as science fiction. It is fitting that North America's Church of Jesus Christ of Latter-day Saints holds a democratic belief that everyone has the opportunity to ascend to a godlike state. Marriage or "sealing" with a person of the opposite sex, either in life or after death, is a necessary qualification to reach this ultimate exultation.

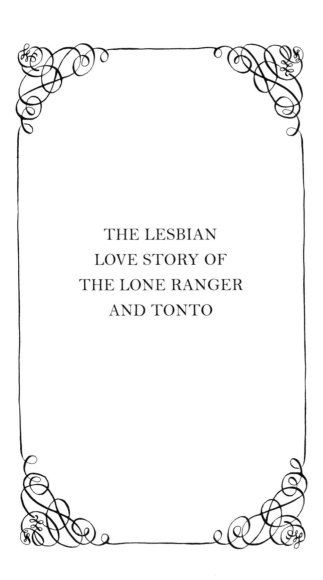

THE LESBIAN
LOVE STORY OF
THE LONE RANGER
AND TONTO

WHAT happens when the Lone Ranger takes off the mask? When the fabric slips and rips and shifts? What happens when the mask falls, leaving her naked between the bridge and the brow?

Well, it turns Tonto on. Tonto, who's not Tonto yet. Tonto, the butchest woman of the Sierra Madre, who left her parents behind to throw tomahawks in a circus sideshow. Tonto, who could eat glass, swallow fire, and grow a beard to boot, who did so with pleasure, and was in fact doing just that when the circus got busted. When the stranger rode into town, white horse-flesh between thighs, hat and belt worn low.

The Lonely Ranger! Here to expose the grift, the graft, the ballyhoo, all the while holding tight her own secret, her own illusion. She had a job to do: laying bare the evil of tricks and trickery, the un-American nature of games of chance. "You have to work hard to get nothing. You can't just get nothing for nothing easy."

Except Tonto, who's not Tonto yet. Tonto

was easy. Or Maria, as she was called then. Not that Maria was her real name, the name given her by her tribe and family. But this is a western, and it seems that in every single western, every single brown-haired, brown-eyed, brown-skinned woman is called Maria.

Ah, Maria. All curves and cream and fireworks. Easy on the surface, like soft-warm griddle cakes, with creases that spread and were sweeter than corn syrup. Easy to rest your head against and cry: for your mama, for the girl you'd been, for fear of what each day would bring.

Easy, and yet when she first tasted and topped the Lonely Ranger, when she first bit, flipped, fucked her, and said, "I, Maria, am your man, and you won't be a lonely ranger anymore," well … the masked hero knew that although talking and crying and touching Maria (later to become Tonto) was easy, any woman with fire in her mouth, who could fuck her big and hard and perfect, was a force to be reckoned with and couldn't possibly be easy all the time.

THE circus tent where this pair made their first bed was burnt, the charlatan carnies were put safely behind bars, and the unscrupulous carnival owner was elected mayor, for that was the way of politics then, as it is today. Maria was out of a job. Maria was no longer wanted. It was time for Maria to go. Whereas the townsfolk extended invitations to the Lonely Ranger, as he-she was still called, in gratitude for inspiring and urging them to purge their hamlet of evil, and they offered up their daughters in marriage as a small token of their appreciation. They did not know that the stranger's tastes had been moved forever from gingham and curls to a big, mannish woman who could snap her lover as easily as kindling with her strong-gentle hands. They did not know how much the masked stranger liked being fucked. They did not know the masked stranger was in fact a woman.

It was this fact, perhaps more than any other,

that kept the Lonely Ranger ranging, running, and you can imagine how far and fast you need to range to escape your own body. Hence it was that this cowboy didn't dilly-dally, nor mosey, but charged here and there on her stallion, Silver, alone.

Maria didn't own a horse. Being a tomahawk-throwing, fire-breathing, glass-swallowing, beard-growing performer in a second-rate circus, she couldn't afford one. She could ride, had ridden since before she could walk. Could skin a horse, for that matter, or even steal one in a pinch.

But the Lonely Ranger didn't think stealing was right. No, the Lonely Ranger insisted that Maria leave the town on foot, and, like the Lonely Ranger, alone.

Needless to say, this made Maria mad. You don't make a woman come without expecting the courtesy of a ride on her horse. Those animals seat two comfortably. And Maria was looking forward to lifting her skirts, and rubbing her clit on the back buckle of the Ranger's chaps as they rode.

Maria was smart. She knew better than to ask for forever. It's such a long time, anyway. But she wouldn't be a secret, either. She was too proud, and everything about her was too big to hide. The tomahawk-thrower knew what she wanted—a lift—and anything less made her spit flames and glass splinters, made the axe arc from her hands....

Fortunately, the masked hero was a good catch, and there, on the main street of town, where everyone could see, but no one would believe, because people only see what they want to, the Lonely Ranger caught that hatchet and cut open her own shirt, exposing a tight nipple, which trembled above her own true heart. Maria was touched, but unmoved. She knew that a heart can be true, but that doesn't prevent its wearer from treating a woman badly. And even though she loved the Lonely Ranger—loved that she was shy, loved that she sang poems, loved that she was brave despite her fears—she also knew there was more than one woman to love in the world, just as there had been many before this lanky, masked one.

AND Maria had loved, hundreds and hundreds and even more times, a great slew of women from Dakota south to the Mexican border. Farm wives, whores, trick riders, and school marms. Seven or eight of her more consuming passions had been pious, black-robed sisters. It could not be said that Maria had a type. These women ranged from sixteen to sixty, rail-thin to gargantuan, pretty to plain to ugly. Some were even willing to leave the worlds of God and men to live in the arms of Maria. But Maria couldn't bear to be someone else's reason. To carry the heart of another seemed an impossible chore in a life that was already so burdened. And anyway, a strange thing happened when these women came to really love Maria. They stepped so close that Maria could barely see them. She was farsighted, and up against her tight, her lovers became all blurry. It's hard to respect someone you can't see clearly. Maria kept moving on.

SHE took the Lonely Ranger's hand, to say farewell and retrieve her tomahawk. She didn't like this feeling, so sore inside. It was time to move on to another circus, to other thighs. The only problem was: she couldn't move. Her tears—and where had they come from?—had made the ground muddy. The same was true of the Ranger. They were stuck, momentarily, in the main street of town, together. And in this moment, this muddy millisecond, the Lonely Ranger reached deep within her pants and removed a small sack of gold. Small, considering it represented the life's work of a father she never knew. Small, considering he got himself killed over it. But large enough to buy a horse. And large enough to make Maria feel, as the Lonely Ranger pressed it to her palm, that maybe this feeling, this soreness, these tears tripping up her feet, were part of something soft and small about herself. Something true.

That night the Lonely Ranger and Maria left

the town together, each carried by a fine stallion. They travelled in silence, surprised by what had passed between them, a little embarrassed, and pondering what it might mean. They travelled until they had to touch each other again, which wasn't long at all.

WHICH brings us to the story of how Tonto was born. The Lonely Ranger, masked "man" and defender of law and order, knew that to continue on the trails with such an obvious bull-dagger, such a well-hung dyke, such a woman who clearly wanted other women and knew what to do with them … it was asking for trouble. Until now the grateful citizenry had turned a blind eye to the Lonely Ranger's slender waist, privacy around toilet habits, and monthly mood swings. A good man was hard to come by in the Wild West. Proclivities were tolerated, up to a point. And that point might well be Maria.

For if the Lonely Ranger were to roam with a larger-than-life lesbo, would it not beg the question? Could these two be birds of a feather? Together? Needing a hiding, a hanging, a real man? The only way the Lonely Ranger could continue to pass as "he" would be to wed Maria. Settle down. Stop ranging. Start a family. Build a happy home.

Which was overlooking entirely that Lonely learned right and wrong and how to shoot in back of the whorehouse where she was raised, but didn't know a thing about farming and building and making a baby inside another woman. Besides, the masked crusader had worked hard at her profession. It might not sound like much to some people, but vanquishing evil made her smile, and she'd be damned if she'd give it up. She couldn't. It was who she was: the Lonely Ranger. Although she wanted Maria, and needed her, too.

It seemed that the only solution was for them both to live as "he," for Maria to become the loyal Indian guide, perhaps: in the background, unnoticed, escaping detection. And although, even then, people were beginning to ask, "What's that smart Indian doing with the dumb white guy?", if they were very careful, if Maria would consent, maybe they could pull it off.

Of course the Lonely Ranger was not the first to think these thoughts. They had galloped in and out of Maria's mind hours before. No one in that town would have sold her a horse, at any price. Women didn't own things. The Lonely Ranger had had to haggle on her behalf. The Lonely Ranger, who was no more man than she. A change was in order. And being the loyal Indian guide was ridiculous enough to amuse her for a while. From her work with the sideshow, Maria knew that if you give people an illusion they understand, they'll believe it. And Maria knew survival, and was old enough that survival didn't hurt her great pride.

AND so the Ranger need not have worried, that night in the white spruce grove, when she asked Maria, not to be her woman, but to be her man. Her sidekick. Buddy. Pal. To be Tonto. An awful word. To make it sound not like it is. To keep the world away. Because what was important to those two women, at that moment, was that they knew.

They knew that when the stars came out, Tonto rode the not-lonely-at-all Ranger. Tonto made the hero weep with love. It was Tonto who could split a hair or a skull with her tomahawk, and would for her woman lover; Tonto who was strong, and understood that the Ranger was weak, afraid, and hiding behind the lie of a mask; Tonto who lit their campfires with her breath.

And it was Tonto who said, "How," to everyone she met, and never meant hello, but silently, laughingly, asked, "How is it that this charade pleases you? How is it that your world is more real than mine? And how is it that we can work and love so hard, but as women our names are never remembered?"

The Lone Ranger *was a radio drama created in 1933 by Fran Striker, inspiring many spin-offs, including comic books, movies, and a hit television series that aired from 1949 to 1957.*

When asked about the character of Tonto, Striker replied, "I invented him so the Lone Ranger would have someone to talk to." Although the word "tonto" means "stupid" in Spanish, Italian, and Portuguese, the series justified the choice by explaining that Tonto was of the Potawatomi nation, and named "wild one" in his indigenous language.

Striker created a detailed credo for the show, to guide the actors in their portrayals. Within the world of the Lone Ranger and Tonto, the characters needed to believe:

- *that to have a friend, a man must be one.*
- *that all men are created equal and that everyone has within himself the power to make this a better world.*
- *that God put the firewood there, but that every man must gather and light it himself.*

- *that a man should make the most of what equipment he has.*
- *that all things change but truth, and that truth alone lives on forever.*

MISS GRAY'S
MARVELLOUS
TRUTH MACHINE

HERE was a time when astrologers were astronomers. And yet another, several hundred years later, when magicians built robots. Even the American military, not so long ago, considered making circus performers the very first astronauts. Out of alchemy and magic comes science. And then science says, "Here I am!" As if it should get a medal. As if it runs the joint. As if it has from the beginning, and we've just been too dumb to notice. But mystery was here long before, and imaginings aren't going anywhere soon.

THE dance school was owned and operated by a grey woman—of hair and name—accompanied by a phonograph. She called it "Astrodust Studios," for Miss Gray had studied her Greek and wanted to convey a more classical approach than mere "Stardust" would evoke. Six evenings a week she taught ambitious adults how to waltz and foxtrot. They had been immigrants, farmers, miners, and factory workers, born poor or in a faraway land. But beneath her pressed tin ceiling, they were reinvented as befit their new professions: merchants, grain traders, cattle barons, and more—the middle class. Their children would never know a life of callouses. They were sent to Miss Gray from a young age in preparation for their society debut.

Miss Gray was capable of moulding young men and women out of pimpled teens. But the real teaching was with the little ones. Children know right from wrong without being told, even when they pretend otherwise. Their notion of truth is bigger than judicial law or even the rules of physics. Words like "should" or "science" mean little, and all experiments have the potential to create magic, especially in the hands of a gifted teacher. Not that anyone *expected* magic in Wichita, but children can't help but hope. And in Miss Gray—Methodist, unmemorable, unmarried—they found magic's glory and its teeth.

THE spark of invention catches in the strangest ways. At Astrodust Studios it strikes up in tap dancing. The sound of the mighty machine nailed to the soles of tiny feet. Faster than imaginable. Noisier than imaginable! Speed and power beyond the clackity-clack of trains and typewriters, telegraphs and machine guns. Flying feet. Modern feet. Feet that could dance right out of Kansas wearing a smile.

MISS Gray was a modern woman. She signed a petition that might someday allow her to vote. She even attended a séance once. When she got headaches, she took a pill. Most of all, she believed things would get better. It was just a matter of time before Christianity and technology solved everything, and vanquished all sin. In the meantime, with a dash of inspiration and two handfuls of grit, a person could achieve almost anything.

At forty-seven, Miss Gray knew marriage was off the plate. In Europe, thousands of men were dying daily. Hers was a problem of supply and demand, and of timing. And yet she'd managed fine thus far. Orphaned at sixteen and teaching school the same year. Teaching thousands of children and loving them, too. She couldn't imagine how, in having her own, she could have loved more. Or worked harder. Lying on small, hard beds in Superintendants' homes, hitching up the horses at six, shovelling coal at seven, and seeing her breath hang frozen in clouds all day, long after the children went home at three-thirty. So what a wonder money was, and what it could bring you! A life's savings of three hundred dollars. Warmth. A parlour with a settee where she could think her own thoughts. And a dance studio where she could teach pleasure and joy and beauty.

And yet she wanted more than this, for few people are so easily satisfied. Her father William's nickname had been Ten Dollar Bill, because he was always saying, "If I just had ten dollars …" and she was no different. Only the amount had changed. Miss Gray harboured secret ambitions for wealth, fame, and even a magnificent new her. She imagined herself becoming a teacher of teachers, a philanthropist, a world traveller; someone who threw parties; someone who made something out of nothing. No matter that it sometimes felt as if everything had already been invented. Life Savers, neon, the zipper…. Miss Gray knew that if she persevered, she'd eventually strike upon an idea that would catch. Miss Gray would make something that would change the world and herself to boot.

From a young age, she had been acquainted with the wonder of electricity. Her earliest memory was of the day her parents took her to town for a demonstration of an electric light. It was as magical as going to any circus. So beautiful and mysterious. Years later she saw a broken phonograph in a shop and begged her father for it. The tinkering began. She quietly fixed things, sold them and bought more. Learning as she went, she jury-rigged new objects from combinations of parts. An electrical heating coil could be transformed into a hair dryer. A cooking ring might make a good bathtub warmer. Nothing was terribly useful or safe, but it was always interesting.

As a dance instructor, she often had to repair her own Victrola when it went on the fritz. There were many different models, breakdowns, shocks, and flaming curtains, but she learned as she went and somehow kept machine and music playing. One day, the record player was being particularly cranky. She slapped its side and cursed, and, just as she was about to hunt for the screwdriver to eviscerate it once again, a strange thing happened. It talked back. Oh, not with words. That would be too Victorian! But its tone was clear. The Victrola was as cross as she was! Miss Gray stopped short and considered. She tried another tack. Over the next few hours she spoke kindly and harshly, humbly and cruelly, sweetly and vexingly, until she could scarce utter another sound. And incredibly, depending on what she said, the machine would emit a high-pitched whine, a middling modulation, or a terrible, low rumble.

At first Miss Gray wondered if she was contacting the dead. The realms of Spiritualism and technology were not necessarily at odds in her mind. But through the night it became clear that the voice of the Victrola was not that of her late father, or other spirits, dear or malevolent. Curiously, amazingly, the machine was responding to *her* mood, her disposition, her meaning.

Well, Miss Gray wondered, if the Victrola could read her emotions, perhaps it could also sense when she was lying. And if so, maybe the pitch of its reply could signal the truthfulness of a statement. Maybe the Victrola could be tuned to truth. Miss Gray almost swooned. Think of the applications! Political candidates, suitors, bad children, criminals: all could be caught in perjury or fabrication. Why, the very existence of the machine would cow society into straight-dealing!

Chicanery, deceit, and prevarication would be things of the past, signalling a return to Eden.

Miraculously, Miss Gray had invented a truth machine. And she knew that truth was powerful. She pictured her name in schoolbooks alongside those of Jesus and Newton and Edison.

OF course, refinements were required. It took several years, but Miss Gray could increasingly tune out the mid-range and get a clear-cut answer five out of nine times. Her pupils helped in this development phase. Some were quite skilled fibbers, and truth was as fun to play with as skipping rope or tap shoes. A small cadre of experimenters was selected for the task—the senior girls' class, ten- to thirteen-year-olds. They enjoyed the intrigue of a secret, of going to Miss Gray's parlour after class, of making up fantastical whoppers and divulging their deepest truths, all of which were recorded by Miss Gray in sombre black notebooks. All the secrets, all the lies, all the results. Sometimes the girls would try to catch the machine out. Ever more extravagant fabrications, ever more intimate truths spilled onto the Turkish carpet in Miss Gray's room. "I did receive a feather from an Indian Chief, really I did!" Although the machine could sometimes be fooled, Miss Gray could not.

But having children to her room—for secrecy was imperative, lest someone steal her invention—was unexpectedly humiliating for Miss Gray. She didn't own anything beyond four dresses, a decent coat, and the few household items that furnished her abode. She called it a parlour, but under the bureau was a slop pail, her Turkish rug was woven in North Carolina, and the threadbare settee served as a bed. Miss Gray had draped the furnishings with scarves and painstakingly painted oak grain on the raw pine floors. Although her desires far outstripped her means, she did her best to make a gracious life. But the girls' curious eyes seemed to catch on every cracked cup, and this made Miss Gray unusually sharp during the truth machine sessions.

Of course, to the children, the parlour was a wondrous place. They were chosen. They were Miss Gray's special friends, and together they were creating an invention to rival the cotton gin and the steam train. They loved telling tales. Most of all, they and they alone were allowed to see the human behind their teacher. The idiosyncrasy of each cracked cup bound them closer to her. Beyond that, the cracks had no meaning at all. So Miss Gray's change in temper was confusing. Miss Gray had taught their feet to strike and blur and soar. Miss Gray was the only person they had ever met who *encouraged* them to make as much noise as possible. So it was hurtful and peculiar when Miss Gray would snap, "Don't touch that."

Nonetheless, she served them biscuits and she listened. None of those little girls could rightly say an adult had ever properly done that before, either. At home later, some of them let slip that they had taken tea with the teacher and were creating a marvellous machine, but no one paid much mind. The activities of little girls and a withered woman hardly mattered. In other words, despite Miss Gray's uncharacteristic temper and the girls' natural loquaciousness, testing proceeded without a hitch for quite some time.

THE problem began when the girls ran out of things to say. And this is where the plot turns; where the promise of invention becomes monstrous. The machine that is meant to catch lying begins to teach lying. The spinster who sought fortune finds disgrace.

At first Miss Gray thought the children were beset by boredom, or worse, judgment. Perhaps the novelty had worn off. Perhaps they recognized the meanness of her life, and wanted release from it. Perhaps they were afraid it was catching. Finally Shirley Ervin blurted the truth: "I've told you everything, Miss. And I can't imagine anything more. You've got all my secrets already, more than I knew I had. And I've made up everything else there is to make."

Of course! She had exhausted her subjects. She just needed new girls! A bigger sample would hasten development, not to mention lend greater credence to her findings. Secrecy be damned. She stopped taking tea with the seniors and invited the much more numerous juniors to her parlour. Miss Gray was close to filing a patent. Manufacture might be less than a year away.

Almost immediately, the tap dancing of her former experimenters faltered. Ellen Huffaker's mother dropped off a note saying Ellen had decided not to continue. And the girls who remained limped along. The sparks that had flown from their toes and eyes dimmed. Rhythms dragged. Form deteriorated. Smiles, an essential component of any tap dance, became reluctant, pained, or absent altogether.

Although she was distracted by her life as an inventrix, Miss Gray was still a teacher to her boots. She laid gunpowder on the floor to surprise and delight the girls. She ran contests for speed and accuracy, awarding precious gold stars. She had them pretend they were insects and horses. She scolded and praised. All of her teaching arts were applied to the problem, but the little girls remained listless. Finally, after weeks of tepid tapping, Ada Dilley gathered her courage and asked for them all, "Miss, what have we done? Why don't you want our visits anymore?"

Miss Gray was dumbfounded and answered truthfully without thinking, "But girls, you simply weren't good at it anymore." Nellie Patterson started crying right there on the spot and hiccupping, too. The hiccups stayed for a fortnight, and were the first strange symptom that would be Miss Gray's undoing. But Miss Gray, blinded by the promise of her invention, missed the signs.

The girls developed tics, twitches, and outbreaks of obscenity, both in language and gesture. They lied at home and at school; they lied well. Most of all they lied about what went on in Miss

Gray's parlour. They feared for their secrets in her notebooks. They had liked being special and hated the inverse. Miss Gray was a witch! She made them strip naked and speak with the devil through a machine. Miss Gray tore the skin around their fingers and drank their blood. She promised them things. Things of which only a twisted spinster could dream, and not a bunch of little girls: the love of an Arab prince, fame, money. They said Miss Gray promised them the world in exchange for their youth. And she did look younger, now that you mention it, quite a bit younger than she had a few years ago. How quickly she was undone.

In the dance class, the girls were each different and each dear. But in the parlour with the pine floor, she saw them as her judges, and that is what they became. Together, the twelve formed a mass, faces distorted and fingers extended in accusation. The mob always becomes faceless, its motives unknowable beyond a kind of animal fear. There is no need to itemize its treachery here. It wasn't personal.

THE three hundred dollars Miss Grey had saved through a lifetime of privation went to lawyers. The truth machine was called as a witness, whined hideously, and was destroyed. Acquitted but destitute, she bought a train ticket to Chicago. With little more than her dresses, she thought maybe she could begin again. She wasn't happy about it, but what else could she do? Modern times promise the world: luxury, ease, the secrets of the universe. But they can just as easily crush a person under the wheels of change.

Her seat in the third-class carriage put her next to a gentleman. Or perhaps he was just a man, but he carried himself with dignity, and who was she to quibble? He was no great looker but pleasant enough; a bit of a braggart, but he shared his lunch. He was travelling the nation, peddling his invention: the toaster. He was amazed she hadn't heard of it. Where had she been? Hundreds had been sold to restaurants from New York to

Salt Lake. The only problem was it cooked just one side of the bread at a time.

As the steam engine jostled and cloaked all that she owned in soot, Miss Gray thought, "I can fix that." It might not merit a mention in the history books, but it was something. The journey wasn't long from Wichita to Chicago, from truth to toast. At the age of fifty she married, and made her husband a rich and famous man.

MODERNITY is a funny thing. We can't see "now" at all. We think we're in it, but already it has passed us by. All we can do is point to yesterday as an example and say, "See how new we are?" And with this newness, like science, there is a feeling of, "Finally we're here!" and "This is where everything has been leading," and "Of course it will remain like this for a very long time." Even though by the time we have thought these thoughts, everything has already changed again.

No wonder people dig in their heels, tighten their corsets, or say things like, "If God had wanted me to fly, He'd have given me wings." It all becomes too much. Superstition (which is not magical at all) seems a safer place to hang one's hat than the blistering pace of change.

Technological innovation in the late 1800s and early 1900s was explosive. Thomas Edison alone produced 2,332 patents for inventions as varied as the incandescent light bulb, the phonograph, railway signals, nickel-plating, the alkaline battery, and poured concrete construction.

In 1913, Lloyd and Hazel Copeman patented the flip-flop toaster that turned a slice of bread, allowing it to be cooked on both sides in succession. In 1919, Charles Strite incorporated a timer, springs, and heating coils into this machine, so it would toast both sides simultaneously. This invention, coupled with sliced bread (made popular in 1930 by the Wonder Bread

Company), led to pop-up toasters becoming a necessary appliance in every home.

In the twentieth century, the proliferation of technology was transformative, but did not necessarily affect social inequities.

"Mass hysteria" has afflicted females at different times in North America's history, dating from the witch trials of Salem, Massachusetts (1692), to the "cheerleader hysteria" of LeRoy, New York (2011–12). Groups of young women succumb to similar symptoms, such as tics, fits, outbursts of obscenity, and physical impairment. Also called conversion disorder and mass psychogenic illness, it is usually blamed on the demons of the day, be they witchcraft, pollution, or the current economic recession. The phenomenon tends to strike high-status young women within a community and spread to those of lesser status.

It has been posited that these clusters of illness reflect variable neurotoxic responses to contaminants. Alternately, "mass hysteria" may subconsciously present a collective opportunity to let go of control and freely rage. Perhaps empathy or a human inclination *for conformity allows this experience to be shared. Or perhaps "infectiousness" is simply permission.*

THE HEADLESS WOMAN
AND HER
SWORD-SWALLOWING MAN

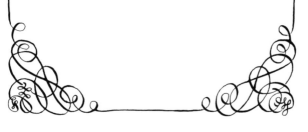

HE romance of the headless woman and her sword-swallowing man began, like so many others, in a bar. He noticed her immediately: long legs, bare arms, the kind of torso that had once stopped traffic. And beyond that nothing. A certain *je ne sais quoi* where her head might have been. A clear view to the bartender stocking the icebox. Open space. The sword-swallowing man liked what he saw. The headless woman's looks, and her lack of looks, were intriguing, to say the least. There was an air of mystery about her and, at the same time, something strangely familiar.

Perhaps she reminded him of the parts he had glimpsed as a young boy, eye pressed to the crack of the changehouse wall. Faceless flashes of nipple and belly and flank that made him feel so good, he feared he was dying.

Of course, that was many years before he became a sword-swallowing man. So many in fact that, as he stood in the bar admiring the woman without a head, he had almost forgotten what it was like to be afraid. Sabres, machetes, and foils of all description had since slid down his throat, and with them the lesson that one moment's fear— just a small tightening of the esophagus—could be fatal. Fearlessness was just part of the sword-swallower's job. And the same way that fire-breathers never smoke in bed and tightrope-walkers never look down, the sword-swallower's lack of fear had become habit. Simply part of who he was. Good in a life-or-death situation. Good at sports. A lady's man.

Although frankly the headless woman didn't notice him at all, until he stood beside her and asked if she wanted a drink. Until that moment she had been lost in thought, contemplating a career change. The headless woman act was going nowhere, fast. Not content with mere headlessness, audiences increasingly wanted more. "Saw her in half," "Throw knives at her," "Make all of her disappear," they chanted, as if headlessness was wearing thin. Headlessness was no longer enough.

As the sweat trickled down her glass, she thought of when, years ago to impress a boy, she had first severed her head and left it in a locker at the bus depot downtown. It had seemed like a lark then, being headless. A party trick. A way to stand out in the crowd.

And yet it was much more than that. A weight had been lifted from her shoulders. The painful, irreconcilable differences between what she saw and what she felt were eliminated. And in the eyes of men she had gone from being pretty to perfect. It was a marketable quality, and previously she had had none.

Needless to say, the key to the locker was forgotten, then lost. Life went on without her head. And she couldn't help but wonder, even if she went now to retrieve it—for surely it was in a warehouse somewhere full of unclaimed articles—perhaps it wouldn't fit. She was not the same person who had left her head behind. And who knew what her head had been up to? It was likely that if they ever were to meet, they would look upon each other as strangers.

This was a problem, she realized, when it came to considering job options. If her opportunities were few, twenty years before as a girl with a head, then they were even more dismal now as a woman—all body—approaching forty.

"Perhaps there's a future in massage therapy," she wondered, that Saturday night in the crowded bar. While the sword-swallower swaggered and the icebox was stocked, the woman without a head thought not of love but of employment.

LOVE is easy to start, hard to finish, and like falling down stairs in-between. The headless woman and her sword-swallowing man bumped along, and bumped plenty against each other, too. They were not unique.

They loved each other, they irritated each other. They bought things, they fought about money. They cried when they came, cried when they were apart, made love, made dinner, made plans, got used to the feelings, and fantasized about other things.

The headless woman would lie awake beside her sword-swallowing man and imagine swallowing his swords herself. The metal running liquid down her throat. Hot or cold? Would it hurt? Could she take it? The funny feeling of the sword-tip hitting bottom, like having too much sex or swimming for too long. And maybe if she laughed or cried or tried to scream, the sword would slice straight out, like *hara kiri* in reverse.

These thoughts and others like them—hanging from a trapeze by her teeth or putting her head into the mouth of a lion—were powerful enough to make her come without touching herself, quietly, as she lay awake beside her sword-swallowing man. She didn't consider herself unfaithful. After all, they were acts performed by a body part she did not have. She reasoned, "It isn't me tasting the knife metal, it isn't me dangling by the skin of my teeth above the crowd, not me choking on the wild beast's spit. No, it's just my head." And at the same time she knew she was truly lying.

THE night they met in the smoky bar, she thought he knew a thing or two. Thought he had smarts and strength and savvy. That he had an edge. He swallowed them, after all.

She couldn't know then that inside her sword-swallowing man was something more frightening: only open space, for his knives to pass easily through. It was the same open space he saw when he looked at her, the same open space he moved in as he walked through the world. He met no resistance. He could afford to be fearless. Everything about him inside and out was clean and clear and empty.

Whereas her insides, her world, even the area above her shoulders where her head should have been, was far, far from vacant. It whined like fluorescent lights. It bit her when she wasn't looking. Sometimes the hum was boring. But still it was real. She didn't like to think about it too much, but the headless woman had always been surrounded by peril. She wasn't crazy or paranoid or making it up. Every voice she had ever heard told her it was true. "It" being the myriad of awful things that can happen, have happened. She knew there were good reasons to be scared, that the world was scary.

She added the sword-swallower to the list. That way the quarrels and threats, fights and bruises made a kind of sense. To be caught in the washing-machine tumble of his fists and feet became a full-time job. She hung on as best she could and called it passion. Hanging on gave her purpose.

WHEN she was a girl, the headless woman thought the perfect job would be to wonder why. She used to spend a lot of time wondering why anyway. It would be great to be paid for it. And it would fulfill a useful function. Lots of questions were unanswered. People got tired of asking their own questions themselves. They could farm that work out to someone else—her, perhaps—who had wondering experience.

But the headless woman didn't wonder as much now as she once did, and if she had had children she might have said things like, "That's just the way it is," and "Because I say so."

When she found her sword-swallower in bed with Mrs. Zeppole of high-flying fame, she didn't wonder at the reason for it. Besides, he told her. "I needed someone to look in the eye. I needed someone to talk to." It made sense that her deficiencies pained him. His pained her, too.

WHEN your every breath is filled with knowledge of all the evil, hurtful ways you can be screwed and screwed over, it's almost a relief to feel a bit of that pain. To be shot out of a cannon. To open your skin with a knife. And then you can say, "See, see, I'm not crazy. This is how it is. This is how it is every day."

So when the pain stops, it takes some getting used to. The headless woman took a bottle of stomach pills. They were handy. They were all that the sword-swallower had left behind.

YEARS ago, when the headless woman began performing, a nurse was required to be in attendance to revive the many swooners and those who would faint dead away. The talker would describe in vivid detail the automobile accident that had left this shapely beauty with nothing above the shoulders, and the miracle of science that had made her the marvel she was today. She was a genuine freak: no mirrors or masks or sleight of hand. And although the story of how she came to headlessness was pure showmanship, no matter.

The proof was in the pudding. She could make them scream. She could make them run away.

But that was before. When there was still wonder and wondering left. Before people had seen it all. Before her love fell flat. Before she took stomach pills to forget herself and her sword-swallowing man.

And was he her sword-swallowing man? Or Mrs. Zeppole's? Do we ever really understand each other? Are we ever fully taken? Or do we slide in and out, sometimes cleanly, sometimes messily, lighting each other up from the inside or scarring the length? Our gag reflex eliminated by months and years of will and practice.

SHE happened to catch the sword-swallower on late-night TV but changed the channel. That motivational stuff was as dull as dishwater; coming from him it seemed particularly hollow. She considered writing a letter of complaint to the station but knew she wouldn't bother. Really, it didn't matter.

The headless woman had regrouped. She trained poodles into a half-decent dog act. Her name changed frequently from "Lovely" to "Talented," "Sweet" to "Delightful." It was a slow process, but quite possibly she was happy. And somehow wonder crept back.

Sometimes she still imagined the knife blade slipping out from inside, like *hara kiri* in reverse. She wanted to plunge her hands into the warm intestines to read them, to make sense of it all. But that would not happen and thank goodness, too. She wouldn't want to clean that up. And although losing a few more body parts at this point in life might not seem like much to some people, she had grown attached to herself. No, the mess of her innards remained firmly in place, a knot without end, a tangle without answers.

She got up off the couch to make herself a snack. Since taking the stomach medication, her appetite had been excellent. Dogs curled around her ankles as she walked to the fridge. She stood over the sink, looked out into the night, and ate.

Phineas Taylor Barnum (1810–1891) was a newspaperman, temperance activist, impresario, abolitionist, philanthropist, elected official, and co-founder of the largest, most extravagant circus the world had ever seen. He is credited with inventing the first sideshow in 1871, featuring displays of historical items, peculiar natural history artifacts, and live acts involving human and animal performers. Sideshows became an essential part of travelling circuses, fairs, and carnivals for over one hundred years.

Typical sideshow performances included working acts (skilled performers such as magicians, sword-swallowers, and fire-eaters) and freak shows (human oddities no less adept at working an audience). Freaks could be born (such as three-legged men, conjoined twins, and bearded ladies) or made (such as tattooed or "illustrated" men, fat women, and human skeletons).

Others, called Geeks in sideshow parlance, entertained with sensational acts, such as biting the heads off of live chickens. Artificial monstrosities, like mermaids and snake-girls, were also available for perusal. Audiences were not put off by questions of authenticity and attended in huge numbers even if something was a proven hoax. In North America, sideshow performers were superstars who had household name recognition in the late nineteenth and early twentieth centuries.

Despite objections from the performers themselves, these amusements came to be viewed as exploitative in the latter part of the twentieth century, and largely disappeared from mainstream carnivals by the 1980s.

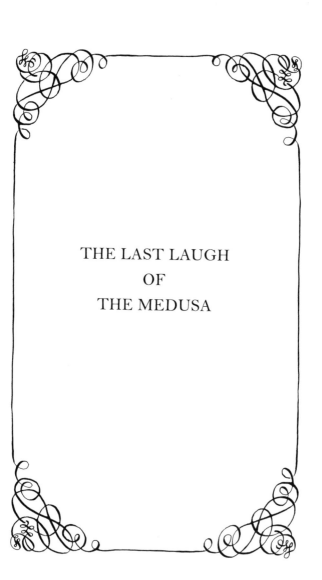

THE LAST LAUGH
OF
THE MEDUSA

MY parents made Goodland their home because of its inexpensive real estate, good gardening soil, and absence of anything remotely Turkish. In fact, Goodland is perhaps most notable for its absence of many things. Situated on a treeless plain, it lacks geographical features, municipal monuments, or indeed anything to mark it as remarkable or unique. It boasts no peculiar rock formations, wildlife, or weather. There are no war memorials, statues of giant turtles or potatoes, or even an eccentric lawn ornament display. Daunted by the challenge of filling the vast prairie, the prudent townsfolk have striven to maintain in Goodland a sense of void—and not only in the physical appearance of the town. The existence of the unusual or the unexplained is emotionally and philosophically negated by almost every man, woman, and child. Hence crime is low and miracles are few, making Goodland a good place to raise a family.

The late 1950s were a notorious time for

conformity, and nowhere was that more evident than in the town of my birth. Equally white souls took part in equally wholesome bonspiels, auctions, and church suppers. As swarthy immigrants of non-Presbyterian faith, my family was not invited. So alien did we seem to the people of Goodland that no attempt at peer pressure was ever made. The life of the community went on around us, at a safe distance.

But this isolation is a faint memory compared to the smell of my mother's cheese pies, or the sound of my father's voice as he told stories of vengeful gods and goddesses. Our kitchen was the centre of my world. As an only child, I was allowed to bask in the full power of my parents' love. I was their hope for the future, their dream of a new world. I was somebody. Sitting on my mother's lap, I learned that Jesus died for me, Opheliah. Sitting on my father's lap, I learned pride. I was a Papadopoulos. I was a Greek. I was a descendant of Zeus.

The idyll of my childhood was unblemished

and would have remained so, had the Cuban Missile Crisis and mounting Cold War hysteria not allowed Goodland's collective denial to reach its zenith. Difference in that town, on November 12, 1962, simply did not exist. The vortex created in the minds of Goodland's citizens was so powerful that my parents were sucked into it, never to be seen again. Also reported missing that day were Li Lo and his wife, proprietors of Café Air Conditioned, and an unlucky travelling salesman with a facial birth defect. They all simply vanished, as if they had never been. I was the only remaining evidence of the tragedy.

Orphaned this way at the age of eight, I learned the importance of fitting in. I feared the black hole that had claimed my parents and actively fought against it. I always changed my underwear. I always ate everything on my plate. I believed what adults told me.

I was fortunate to be adopted by Miss Titus, an elderly spinster and breeder of dwarf hogs. And I became just like everyone else, to the best of my ability. I had no particular passions or foibles. My grades were average. I had neither friends nor enemies. I couldn't resist the thought that I, too, had vanished, but the event had been so unremarkable that no one had noticed, not even me.

I undertook a variety of experiments designed to prove or disprove my existence: not eating, eating too much, cutting. Several near-death experiences reassured me that I was in fact alive. This wasn't particularly good news, but I decided to make the best of it.

On the eve of my grade twelve graduation, Miss Titus's hiatus hernia required her hospitalization. By the next morning she had passed on, and I was once more an orphan. Her last will and testament bequeathed the hogs, the house, and one hundred shares in Manitoba Hydro to her only living relative, her nephew Lesley. I received the household effects and a strongly worded recommendation that I marry Les before I was too old or he found someone better suited to the task. I carefully examined my options before withdrawing seventy-five dollars in life's savings from the credit union and getting on the first Grey Goose bound for anywhere else.

In Manitoba, most roads lead to nowhere, with a few exceptions that lead to Winnipeg. It was in Winnipeg that I ended up. I was eighteen, blessed with neither wealth nor beauty, friendless, skill-less, and with no idea what I'd do next.

ON rare occasions adversity inspires new well-springs of courage. Despite the sad state of affairs, I felt positively exhilarated. I was, after all, free.

From the bus depot I marched, stopping at each business to ask for a job. At last, at the local perogy house, I was successful in obtaining gainful employment.

In no time I had a cozy apartment, real friends, and a sense of fulfillment. What I did was important. I was making the world a better place. I even began taking night courses at Red River College in accounting. I could see debits and credits as perogies not paid for or not eaten; monthly balance sheets as links of sausage, unique unto themselves but together forming a harmonious continuum. I was an A+ student. I was no longer dieting. For perhaps the first time in my life, I was happy.

It is true that I have never been a lucky person. I have often wondered if the gods present me with ill fortune to test me. Or perhaps I am paying for the sins of my kin or a misdemeanour I have unwittingly committed. Whatever the reasons, my happiness was short-lived. What happened next was not exceptional. Worse horrors have happened to many women. And yet it is painful, so I will be brief and use plain language.

My friend and employer Ann was married to a big, jolly man named Burt. One night I was working late, trying to figure out a way to maximize perogy flow and minimize inventory, when Burt came round to pick up his wife. As she cashed out, Burt took me to the back of the shop and raped me. When he had finished, he collected my dear Ann, who had been waiting patiently, and drove her home.

The next morning I returned to the store, battered and confused, to console my friend and be consoled by her. Instead I was handed my separation papers and my final pay.

That's all. That's the end of that story. I finished my courses. I ate little and slept less. I stopped talking.

IT was at this point in my life that I decided to become a man. Not physically—I never dreamt that was possible. But I realized my upbringing had taught me to be passive and not assertive; to play piano and not hockey; to feel too much and take too little. Miss Titus had betrayed me. Ann had betrayed me. Even my mother, in her disappearance, had betrayed me. I hated women. I loathed the feminine. I was committed to being male from here on in.

I realized, however, that before I could become a man, I must become a boy. My childhood had been a complete waste of time. I must begin again. I got a new wardrobe. I caught reptiles and tortured them mercilessly. I spat. I swore. I never cried. I went fishing on weekends and drank beer until I puked. No one could tell me what to do. It was my world. I was one of God's chosen people. I was a male child.

I got a job at a meat-packing plant, driving a forklift. I was making three times what I had earned at the perogy house. I bought my first gold chain.

Notwithstanding my dubious gender, the men at the plant accepted me. We had so much in common. We'd talk about the virtues of a Slant-6 over a V-8 engine, who'd won the game, what a bitch the floor manager was. I think what really endeared me to them was my newfound sense of humour. I'd make farting noises with my armpit. I sang the chorus of "Taking Care of Business" while belching. I bought T-shirts with funny sayings on them. Finally, I belonged. I was one of the boys.

But despite my outward air of self-confidence there lived, deep within me, a tiny voice that said, "I am afraid." I feared that people could see through me and would know that my macho bravado was an affectation I'd assumed for self-protection. Perhaps my female-to-male transformation was incomplete. Or perhaps it is part of being a man, that small voice of self-doubt. I had no way of knowing.

Of course, one of the most popular topics of talk among my buddies was women. Following their lead, I began to hang out in the all-female packing department. Strangely, it irritated these girls when I dominated the conversation and talked constantly about myself. I'd tell them to get me another cup of coffee and they'd remain impassive. Jumbo, our foreman, would wink at the gals and say, "Nice tits," sending them into peals of laughter. When I tried it, I was reported to the plant manager for sexual harassment.

It was at this point that things changed. I was banned from the packing area. A wall of silence met me when I entered a room. My old jokes didn't work anymore. Even my friends would have nothing to do with me. I felt almost as if they were somehow afraid.

Shortly thereafter my employment was terminated, not by management, but by vigilantes. As I came around the outside corner of the warehouse that Friday afternoon, they were waiting for me. Armed with frozen legs of lamb that they held like clubs stood Jumbo, Vincent, Hassam, and Pinkie. "Come here, bull dyke," they taunted. "Come here, cunt."

Obviously my masculinity had been misinterpreted. I did not love women. I just wanted to be a man.

As I faced my impending bludgeoning, I was forced to make a difficult choice. Would I stay and fight, as any proper male would? What was to be gained? The end result would leave me neither virile nor feminine but simply bloodied. In that

moment I rejected the concept of gender altogether. I would adopt neither male nor female
role. I would simply survive.

Quick to put theory into practice, I ran for my
life. I ran until I was safe and continued running
for good measure. I never returned to the packing
plant for either pay or possessions. I still have a
hard time eating that company's meats.

Generally speaking, being neither male nor
female is difficult in this world. How do you get
dressed in the morning? What do you eat for
breakfast? How do you walk down the street?
Without gender, do you in fact exist? Maybe this
was the void I'd feared most of my life. Maybe
this was my personal black hole. Just as my
parents had been swallowed by the small-minded-
ness of a community that had failed to recognize
them, I was being swallowed by my own lack of
definition.

I would get up in the morning and be greeted
in the mirror with a blank image. There was nowhere I could find myself reflected. For what had

I been taught to see, beyond the norm? Just freaks and monsters.

ONLY in my dreams could I change and change and change with ease. In my dreams I could be a boy, a camera, lightning, sword, woman, and myth, simultaneously and in succession. So it was into my dreams that I retreated, though I remained awake. Like a sleepwalker I moved through the next three months, letting images flow over me like a river. The stories and legends that my parents had told me as a child resurfaced during that time, and slowly they began to have meaning. Slowly, slowly, they washed away illusion and began to show who I truly am.

"Was it painful," one might ask, "this process of self-revelation?" To the contrary. Although I hesitate to admit it, an unexpected sensation made the process compellingly pleasurable. Deep, successive orgasms welled up inside me, night and day, making it impossible to worry. I felt unashamedly sensual. True, my desire surprised me. Its strength was unmistakable, immeasurable, *huge*. But I did not hide from it or the images it brought. I felt proud of the power between my thighs. I knew it had the strength to move mountains.

One morning, I awoke with the confused emotions of a newborn: abandonment, anger, anticipation, wonder. The metamorphosis was complete.

As I turned to greet my true self in the mirror, each snaky lock of hair reached out to me. "You're horrible," they said. "You're safe." A smile grew from deep within me and spread like a jack-o'-lantern across my face. My eyes bulged and my tongue grew. I laughed as I realized that now anything was possible. I could go forth into the world simply as me, unquestioned and unassaulted, my resplendent ugliness as my shield.

As I gazed on the face of the Medusa, I felt peace.

SUDDENLY my clothing seemed inadequate. The starched smocks of my perogy days and the plaid shirts of my meat-packing months all seemed beneath the magnificent creature I had become. I took myself to the most expensive women's clothier I knew, into whose windows I'd previously only dared to glance. As I entered, fresh-scrubbed clerks snapped to attention and rushed to supply me with my every wish and whim. I bought only the latest, the 100%, the designer labels, and I was fearless as I paid with money I did not have.

Next, I realized I needed a job. It didn't even occur to me to spend hours waiting in lines at the employment office. Armoured in Alfred Sung, I took a cab downtown to the city's tallest building. I marched into the lobby and asked to see the president of the company. Phones rang, guards bowed, and the receptionist personally escorted me to what felt like the ninety-ninth floor. Doors opened magically before me as I strode into an office larger than my entire apartment and confronted a small, withered man behind a large, granite desk. I would be his personal assistant, I informed him and, entranced, he shook my hand in agreement.

Each day I would use the brisk half-hour walk to the office as an opportunity to go over my personal goals. Once there, I guided the elderly Mr. Taylor through the day like a terrible angel. There were no obstacles we did not brush aside. Lawmakers, stockholders, managers, and staff all magically bowed to Mr. Taylor's will, just as George Taylor bowed to mine.

I would forgo lunch in favour of meditation and Tantric chants, and at 6:00 p.m., as the other employees left for the day, I stayed at my desk, poring over sales profiles and flow charts. I learned every nut and bolt of the industry late at night in that glass tower. I learned so much that, within a year, I knew more than anyone in the company.

This was fortunate, because within a year, dear old Mr. Taylor was dead of a heart attack, locked in rigor mortis behind his granite desk.

My promotion from personal assistant to president was smooth and painless. After the funeral I returned to the office, forgoing the reception. When the other mourners arrived for work the next day, I was already ensconced in Mr. Taylor's office and the stationery had been changed. Not that anyone would have questioned my right to leadership. I was the logical choice for the job. I had simply saved them the formality of asking me.

ASIDE from the larger desk and improved view, very little has changed in my life.

My lack of physical beauty in no way dampens the contentment I feel. I am able to maintain what few assets I have, and am happy to report that I am blemish-free, cellulite-free, and polyester-free.

I strive for a look that *Cosmopolitan* describes as assertively feminine. I am not above perfume and décolletage in the boardroom, for I understand from experience that people cannot accept a powerful woman if she does not at least appear fuckable.

My behaviour is not radically different from when I was trying to be a man. But because I look very much like a woman, with the exception of my snaky hair, it is accepted that I know my place. Since my appearance beguiles, it is assumed that I am not an unnatural monster. They accept me because I let them conquer me in their fantasies. But in reality my business acumen turns them to stone.

Although I let many consider the possibility, I let no man into my bedroom. It is the sacred shrine of my transformation. Besides, the vile bumping and grinding on the perogy house floor remains fresh in my memory and always will. I have no desire to have the performance repeated, however sensitive, or skilled, or heaven-forbid long the Romeo promises it will be.

Now, some would say that working eighteen hours a day, having no interpersonal relationships, and earning a six-digit salary does not constitute a path to fulfillment. I, on the other hand, beg to differ. I trust no one and am betrayed by no one. And I have control over all aspects of my life except one. Perseus.

I know there are many who would like to see my head severed from my neck. It's a dog-eat-dog, hero-slays-monster, kill-the-bitch world. Realistically, my days are numbered.

Although I am willing to fight for life, I do not fear death. The possibilities of forevermore fascinate me. Will my parents be there? Will they even recognize me? Will they be proud? I am not the same as I was when I was a child. There have been so many necessary changes. I regret little.

Finally, I am able to see myself clearly and accept myself for what I am: demanding, single-minded, and even repulsive. My detractors might snigger behind my back. Or cower! But no matter.

I chose this fate; it didn't choose me. I am truly a self-made woman.

In the ancient Greek myth, Medusa is raped by Poseidon and cursed by ugliness for the crime against her. Later, she is decapitated by Perseus, who uses Medusa's snaky head to turn entire armies to stone.

The enduring power of this story may be linked to the prevalence of snaky-haired goddesses in pre-Greco-Roman cultures. In Sanskrit, her name translates as "sovereign female wisdom." In North Africa, Medusa was the destroyer aspect of the triple goddess, the trinity of the time. The Greeks appropriated and undermined the Medusa, usurped her power, and incorporated her into a cautionary tale.

Much later, Sigmund Freud equated decapitation of the Medusa with castration.

In 1979, Margaret Thatcher became the first female leader of the Western world. As British Prime Minister, "The Iron Lady" waged war, crushed unions, and destroyed social programs. Thatcher exemplified some professional women of the era who were determined to crack or negate the glass ceiling by being as aggressive as men, and succeeding on merit.

A FALLING
WOMAN

A WOMAN snaps her heel in a sewer grate. "Damn," she thinks to herself, "those shoes were expensive." She turns and bends down to pick up the broken part, thinking, "Maybe it can be reattached." But she cannot dislodge it. She struggles and struggles, and as she does so, she happens to glance down into a pair of eyes looking up at her. She screams. She lets go of the heel. She apologizes. "Oh, I'm sorry," she says. And she looks again.

She sees a little man beneath the grate: not very little, not like a Barbie doll or even a dwarf, but a regular man who just happens to be short. Unless, she wonders, that is just her perspective, being up above him and all. He smiles, twists the heel loose, draws it down, and puts it in his pocket. "His suit, it must be custom," she thinks. "He must have his own tailor."

As if reading her thoughts, he says, "Italian," and with that he begins to climb down and away, out of sight.

"Wait," she cries. "My heel." The short

gentleman laughs, his voice echoing in the darkness. She threatens, "I'll call the police! I'll have you arrested!" She begs, "I'll give you money!"

Suddenly he reappears. "Money?" He really is rather attractive. And well-groomed, which is so rare in a man. He must be gay. "How much money?" he asks.

"Five dollars. Like a finder's fee. Five dollars? I think that's fair."

He laughs again. One of those really great laughs, genuine, without a hint of irony. "How about two hundred?"

Two hundred dollars? The pair only cost her one-fifty. "Oh, come on…"

At which point a driver leans on his horn and shouts, "Get off the road," for she is crouched in the middle of a side street. Unmoved and unmoving, she looks up and gives the man behind the wheel what she thinks is, what she has practised to be, her withering stare.

"Nice," says the short fellow from below. "Nice."

"Look," she says, appearing reasonable, smiling

winningly, dropping her volume to an empathetic and intimate level. "I'm sure we can work this out. Would you like to join me for a coffee? I'm sure we can come to a friendly agreement."

"No!" the little man snaps. "How much do you have on you?"

"That's none of your...."

"I'll show you mine if you show me yours." And with that he reaches into his suit jacket and removes a bank statement.

She scoffs. "This is meaningless. What are your liabilities?"

"Alas," he smiles, "many. And yours?"

"Well, I've got a broken heel, for one thing." They laugh easily. Are they flirting? She leans closer to get a better look. And he vanishes. He doesn't walk away, climb down, move out of sight. He disappears.

The next day she returns to the sewer grate at exactly the same time and drops a five-dollar bill between the slats. It drifts down into blankness. Nothing happens. Just as she is about to leave, cursing her stupidity and the little man who stole her heel, he appears, reaching a delicate hand up between the grate, palm up. "Thank you," he says. "But it is not enough."

"What do you do down there?" she asks.

"I wait for you." And he is gone. One moment standing there in front of her and the next as if he never was.

The next day she brings ten dollars. "Bring your face closer," she demands. And he tilts it to the sunlight. "He isn't *that* short," she thinks to herself, and returns the next day with a twenty.

Each day for three months she drops larger and larger sums. Once she tries to leave nothing, but then he does not appear. She attempts to plateau at fifty dollars, but again he does not appear. The amounts get bigger. Soon she is writing cheques. She forgets about her heel. One day he calls her "my sweet," another day "my heart," then "my love." They touch fingers and feel each other's breath. And he isn't short at all, anymore.

He wears a new suit each day, because each

day he gets bigger. He becomes tall and broad and huge. His body fills the tunnel.

"This is all I have," she says, as she drops her last credit card, the PIN attached with a yellow sticky note. "I have given you everything, and now you must come up and be with me. Besides, the sewer has grown too small for you."

"No, it is I who have grown large." He smiles and begins to climb down, down. She cries because she knows she has lost him. She rests her face against the sewer grate and weeps. And as she does, he reaches up and deftly rips the chain from around her neck, plucks the diamonds from her ears. And then he is gone.

WHEN the woman was a child she fell into an old well on her grandparents' farm. It wasn't that deep. She didn't hurt herself. She landed at the bottom in a pile of old leaves and rubbish, in a few inches of water. But even though she could hear them calling her name, she couldn't answer.

Now, years later, she avoids crowded spaces. She walks to work and takes the stairs to the eighteenth floor. Her Thigh Master routine, she jokes. Not neurosis, just cheaper than a gym membership.

At the office she watches over a football field of telemarketers. The cubicles stretch almost to the vanishing point. Everything is timed. Every thought, every word. There are standards to adhere to and targets to meet. She is a supervisor. She is both the timer and the timed. Two clocks run inside her, making time and losing time, until the stroke of five when she can begin her descent, her exercise regime, again.

ONCE at Club Med in Cancun, she spent a day rock climbing. She lost all sense of up and down. She simply was in-between the two.

At one point she forgot herself, forgot to pay

attention to the correct sequence of moves, and she began to fall. But the carabiner gripped and the rope held her, dangling but tethered.

A WOMAN falls down a hole. It looks like she may have jumped, may have intended to fall, to do herself harm, but it really wasn't like that at all. It's embarrassing. If she never makes it back to the surface, everyone will wonder why. They'll make up complex psychological reasons, and will look back over the past few months for signs. Which is ridiculous! Not that she can explain it, either. All she knows is that one minute she was walking to work and the next she was tumbling.

Packed earth walls studded with bits of rock fly past her. There is nothing to grab onto and the walls skin her knuckles. A sound comes out of her, a sob, because it hurts. She's afraid. Afraid for a long time. But still she doesn't hit bottom.

Where is she? Some sort of shaft to the

underpinnings of the city? A portal to waste or water or electricity? "Who knows what to wish for?" she wonders. "A wet landing?" Gross. "Electrocution?" She hopes that at the bottom it won't be too painful. Even though she knows it probably will be.

She falls some more and still nothing happens. "Weird," she thinks to herself. "This must be one of those near-death moments when time stands still." It is like being in a bad cartoon, where the exact same landscape keeps going by. After a while it gets boring. "It's funny," she almost laughs. "Most of my life has been like this, either scared or bored."

She has time to consider hundreds of mundane things. She is kind of hungry, but not too bad. If she had her purse, she could eat those sesame snaps she keeps for emergencies. How long has she been carrying those around? She hasn't missed a day of work in three years. Shame to break that attendance record. She wonders if her plants will get thrown out or adopted. Mostly she does nothing, just feels the rushing breeze. It is cooling.

She is glad she has her jacket. Even though she is falling, her outfit still looks good. Even though she is hurtling towards her demise, she's grateful she looks put together.

"You at least think the light would change as I get further from the surface," she thinks. But it doesn't. It's all just dim.

SOMETIMES you hear about a bronze sculpture being stolen from in front of an office building, not because it is art but for the metal. It gets melted down in no time, a perfect crime. No evidence. And with the housing crisis in the States, the same thing is happening there. Whole neighbourhoods, abandoned because people can't pay their mortgages, are stripped of copper wire. So it makes sense that the odd manhole cover or sewer grate would go missing. Metal's expensive.

A Falling Woman

THE woman's job requires "business attire." She wonders what that means anymore. A better brand of track suit? Festive sweaters paired with pocketless trousers? Really, the things she's seen in the workplace…. Whatever happened to standards?

Still, despite being surrounded by Don'ts, she really doesn't understand the Do's. She wants to get noticed and get ahead, but not be too obvious, too much. She buys accessories and returns them. They send the wrong message: old money (smug) or new money (crass) or no money (all wrong). Could her look be described as "spare"? Or "classical"? Maybe "modernist"? No, that's too uppity, too contrived. "Simple"?

The trick is to appear professional yet approachable, up-and-coming, yet one of the gang. She's a team player, but she stands out from the pack. In a good way. She hopes.

Of course there are people over her and people under her. She can work within a structure.

A WOMAN breaks her heel in a sewer grate. She waits and listens and hears it fall somewhere in the darkness below.

Fortunately, she is a rock climber. Or at least she did a course once on vacation. Using all her strength, she drags the metal cover to one side and lowers herself into the hole from the slats. She hangs from the grate. Maybe this wasn't such a good idea. But damn it, she wants her heel. She thinks of Angelina Jolie and Indiana Jones, and swings her feet to find the ladder embedded in the wall.

At the bottom of the hole there are two doors. One leads to a staircase that ascends, switching back and forth as far as the eye can see. The other leads to a staircase that descends. Both are lit by wall sconces. There is no difference, just up and down.

The woman chooses up. She has appointments this afternoon. A friend is dropping by this evening. And rent is due tomorrow. She needs to get back. So she starts to climb, and climbs and climbs until she cannot climb anymore. Then she stops.

She realizes it probably wouldn't have mattered if she had chosen the down staircase. She'd have ended up in the same spot: in-between.

ONE night, the woman comes home from work a little later than usual with two bags of groceries. She unlocks the door, goes inside, puts the bags down, and opens the fridge. That's when she notices: the condiments are all wrong. Everything else is just as it should be, except that she is looking deep into the icebox of someone else's life. Another woman has bought the more expensive mayo and, inexplicably, fish sauce. What do you do with fish sauce? There is no ancient horseradish, no barely used mint jelly, no half-jar of maraschino cherries left over from New Year's.

She instantly understands that she is the victim of identity theft. To an untrained eye nothing has changed. But she can see that everything has changed.

Identity theft probably isn't new, but it feels new. Surely since time immemorial charlatans have impersonated gods and kings and wise men. And who among us hasn't wanted to be more than we are, fibbed at a party about what exactly we do? Data entry? Information systems management! Who among us has not dreamt of leaving town, of reinvention, of disappearing?

Do you remember the CEO in New Zealand who lied on his resume and claimed to have been an NHL referee? What a masterful invention! Who in New Zealand would know hockey? And even if they did, he didn't pretend to have been a player, but rather one of those anonymous striped men who control the play. Someone almost invisible who nonetheless, through a good or bad call, can determine who advances to the Stanley Cup, who becomes immortal, who gets the ring.

A Falling Woman

⤚

A WOMAN follows the same route on her walk to work each day. She has timed all the various options and this one is the quickest. Structure has always served her well. It is a way to proceed. Routine fills time in an orderly way, which is comforting. Or at least it helps.

She wears her work shoes. They aren't the most comfortable but there's something so '80s about the business suit and New Balance look, so American.

She doesn't multi-task as she commutes. She doesn't power walk. She doesn't mentally prep for her day. Walking is nice empty time between home and the office. And so effortless. She doesn't even need to think about it. Sometimes five or ten minutes go by without her remembering what she is doing.

Of course her mind wanders. She remembers the trip to the Planetarium in grade school. And that *National Geographic* article about time–how humans invented it, and how without measurements maybe it wouldn't exist. She thinks about the trips she's taken and whom she's loved, her favourite foods and her grandparents' farm.

She always walks on the same side of the streets, crosses at the same point in each block. So she really isn't paying attention.

The End

PERFORMANCE ARTISTS Shawna Dempsey and Lorri Millan have toured internationally for over 25 years. Their films and videos have screened in venues ranging from the Museum of Modern Art to women's centres in Sri Lanka, and include provocative, humourous works such as *We're Talking Vulva* and *Lesbian National Parks and Services*. Dempsey and Millan's site-specific installations include the creation of video talking heads for ancient Greek sculptures in the Royal Ontario Museum (*Archaeology and You*) and a functioning midway, complete with rides and cotton candy, that closed the nexus of Canada's financial district, Bay Street (*Wild Ride*). They are the authors of the *Winnipeg Tarot Co. Tarot Deck*, *In The Life* (a companion to the film *A Day in the Life of a Bull-Dyke*), and the *Lesbian National Parks and Services Field Guide to North America*. Winnipeg, Canada, the geographical centre of North America, is their chosen home.

A version of "Confession of the Pirate Mary Read" was previously published in *MAWA: Culture of Community, Mentoring Artists for Women's Art*, 2004. A version of "The Headless Woman and Her Sword Swallowing Man" was published in *Short Stories*, Winnipeg Art Gallery, 2002. A version of "Medusa" was published in *Front Magazine* and *Canadian Theatre Review*, 1993.

Nouuelle Decouuerte de Plusieurs Nations Dans la Nouuelle France

MER GLACIALE

Mer Vermeille ou est La Californie par ou on peut aller au Perou au Japon et ala chine

La Nouuelle-Grenade

Le Mexique

LE SEIN